JOJOFU

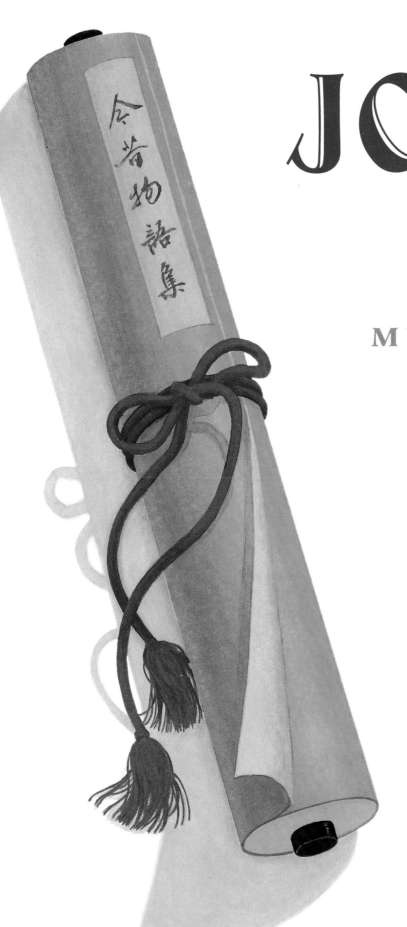

BY
MICHAEL P. WAITE

ILLUSTRATED BY
YORIKO ITO

LOTHROP, LEE & SHEPARD BOOKS
NEW YORK

Jojofu is based on a Japanese folktale taken from the ancient Ima Mukashi scrolls, today known as the Ages Ago Stories. These medieval tales were collected from India, China, and Japan over a period of fifteen hundred years (from about 500 BC to 1075 AD). The original language was a Chinese-Japanese hybrid. "Ages ago" is the traditional beginning for Buddha's birth stories and most Japanese fairy tales. The name Jojofu means "heroine."

Text copyright © 1996 by Michael P. Waite
Illustrations copyright © 1996 by Yoriko Ito
All rights reserved. No part of this book may be reproduced or utilized in any form or by any means, electronic or mechanical, including photocopying and recording, or by any information storage and retrieval system, without permission in writing from the Publisher. Inquiries should be addressed to
Lothrop, Lee & Shepard Books, a division of William Morrow & Company, Inc., 1350 Avenue of the Americas, New York, New York 10019.
Printed in the United States of America
First Edition   1 2 3 4 5 6 7 8 9 10
Library of Congress Cataloging in Publication data was not available in time for the publication of this book, but can be obtained from the Library of Congress.
Jojofu. ISBN 0-688-13660-5.   ISBN 0-688-13661-3 (lib.bdg.)

For Ed and Amy Yamamoto—*watashi no kazoku, watashi no tomodachi*—MW

To My Family—YI

AGES AGO, IN THE PROVINCE OF MUTSU, there lived a young hunter named Takumi. Takumi kept thirty hunting dogs for tracking wild boar and stag in the dangerous mountains. He loved these dogs as if they were his own children, and his very favorite was named Jojofu, for she was the bravest and smartest hunting dog in the land.

One day Takumi packed his hunting bow and sword and set out for the mountains with ten of his strongest dogs. He made all of the dogs follow behind him except for Jojofu, for she could always sense danger and was afraid of nothing.

They climbed high into the wooded hills. Jojofu picked a careful trail through the stones and brambles. Takumi was very surprised when they came to a grassy hillside and Jojofu crossed quickly into the thick forest on the other side.

"Why are you headed into the woods, you foolish dog?" said Takumi. "The hillside is wide open and easy for walking."

But Jojofu just looked back at him and barked, then hurried into the forest. Takumi ran after her, shouting, "No, Jojofu! Come back! This is not the right way!"

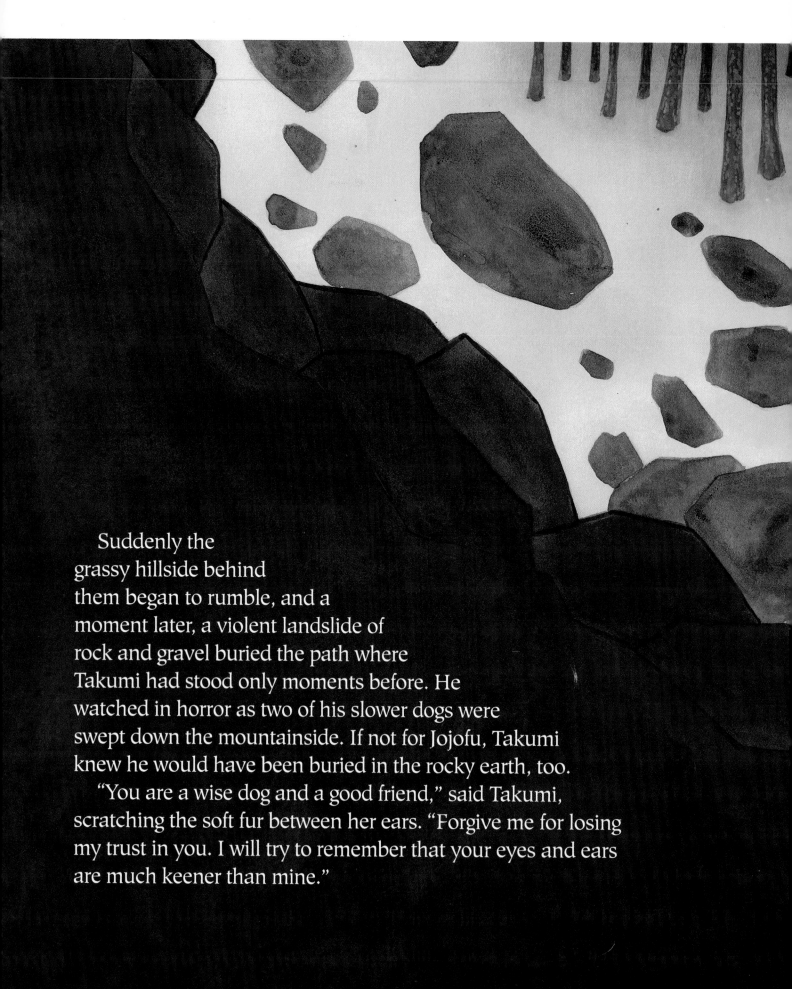

Suddenly the
grassy hillside behind
them began to rumble, and a
moment later, a violent landslide of
rock and gravel buried the path where
Takumi had stood only moments before. He
watched in horror as two of his slower dogs were
swept down the mountainside. If not for Jojofu, Takumi
knew he would have been buried in the rocky earth, too.

"You are a wise dog and a good friend," said Takumi,
scratching the soft fur between her ears. "Forgive me for losing
my trust in you. I will try to remember that your eyes and ears
are much keener than mine."

As the forest grew thicker and darker, Jojofu moved slowly, picking out the safest trail toward the hunting grounds. An eerie gray mist rose from the nearby swamps and crept across the leaves and underbrush. When the mist had become as thick as cobwebs, she suddenly stopped. She turned to her master and barked, nudging him with her nose.

"Why are you stopping here?" said Takumi, feeling very tired. "We must get to the hunting grounds before we camp. Please, Jojofu, hurry along. I am hungry and anxious to sleep."

But instead Jojofu lay down at her master's feet. She nuzzled him softly with her head and barked, refusing to move another inch. Bakana, the most impatient of the dogs, raced ahead into the mist, and Takumi followed.

Suddenly, from somewhere deep in the fog, Takumi heard a frightened yelp. A moment later came the sound of crashing dirt and stones. He cried for the other dogs to stop at once, fearing the worst. Then, using a stick, he poked his way through the mist and felt where the ground came suddenly to an end at the edge of a jagged cliff.

"You have saved our lives for a second time," Takumi said, hugging Jojofu. "Because I believed only my own eyes and ears, I nearly went over the cliff like Bakana. I have learned my lesson. From now on, I will never lose faith in you, no matter what you do!"

By then the forest had grown
very dark, so Takumi built a campfire and
made a bed for himself high in the crook of an
old tree. There were many dangerous beasts in the
forest, but he knew he would be safe up off the ground,
especially with Jojofu sitting among the roots below. After a
dinner of fish and rice, he climbed into his bed and fell fast asleep.

In the middle of the night, Jojofu woke him with a terrible growl. Takumi shook off his sleep and gazed down to see what was the matter. She was staring up at him from the ground below, snarling viciously, her white teeth bared in the moonlight.

"What is the matter?" said Takumi. "Don't you see? It's only me up here."

But the angry dog rose to her hind legs against the tree, snarling and snapping. Froth flew from her jaws, and her eyes were as fierce as fire. Takumi began to worry.

"Maybe she has eaten a poisonous mushroom," he thought. "Or maybe a forest spirit has made her crazy."

Looking around the forest below him, he noticed that all of his other dogs were missing. Something was terribly wrong. Only Jojofu remained at the foot of the tree—and Takumi had never seen her act this way before.

She clawed madly at the tree trunk beneath him and sprang into the air over and over. Her angry snarls echoed throughout the forest and her teeth flashed white with rage.

"She has gone mad!" cried Takumi, growing afraid for his life. He drew out his sword and held it above his head in warning, but Jojofu would not back down. With each leap she rose higher into the air, coming closer and closer to the branches where he sat. What could he do? Would he be forced to kill his dear friend in order to save himself?

Suddenly he remembered his promise. He had told Jojofu that he would never lose faith in her again. Twice today she had saved his life. Twice she had proven her loyalty. Even if a spirit had made her crazy, how could he turn against her now? Takumi trembled as he put his sword back in its sheath. Then he closed his eyes and jumped.

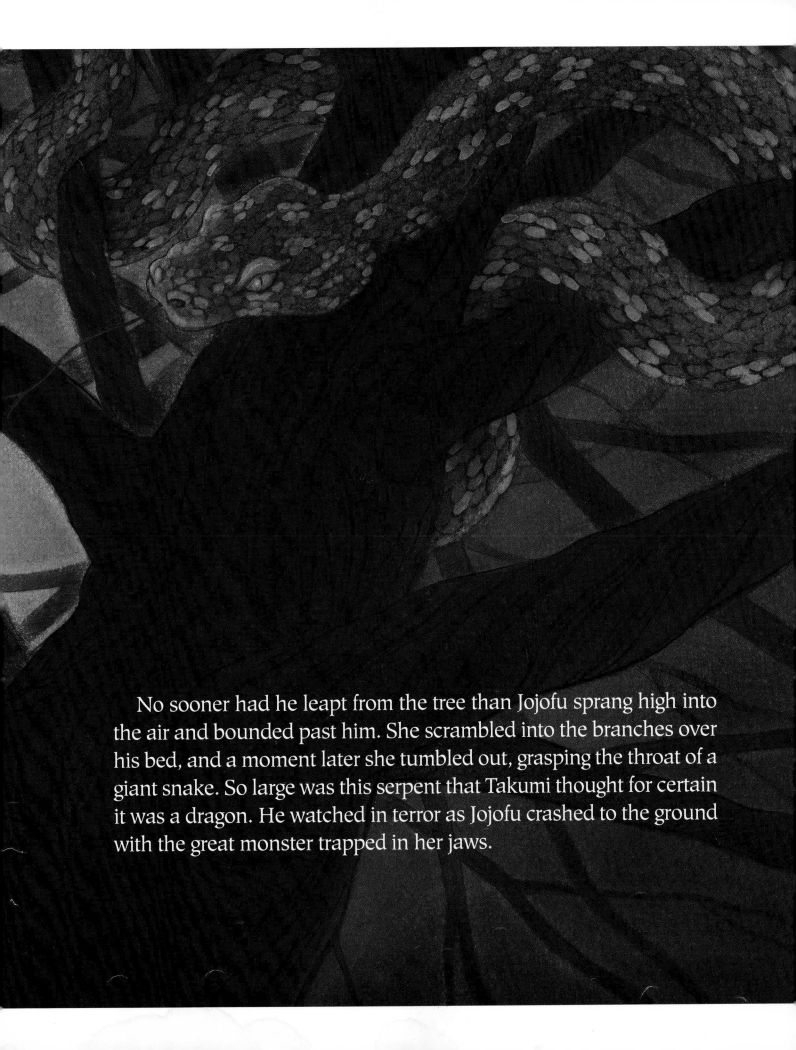

No sooner had he leapt from the tree than Jojofu sprang high into the air and bounded past him. She scrambled into the branches over his bed, and a moment later she tumbled out, grasping the throat of a giant snake. So large was this serpent that Takumi thought for certain it was a dragon. He watched in terror as Jojofu crashed to the ground with the great monster trapped in her jaws.

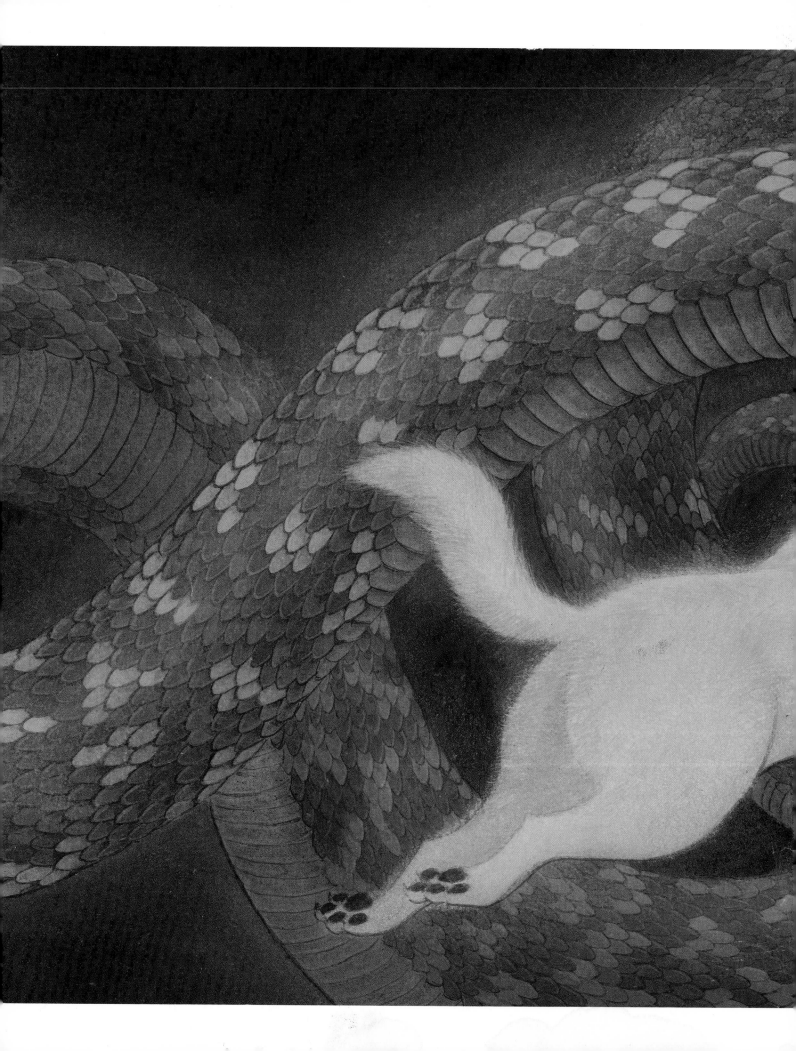

The snake coiled back,
baring its yellow fangs. But
before it could strike, Takumi
came to his senses. He drew his sword
and killed it with a single blow. Then he fell
to his knees and hugged his bravest dog.
"You have saved my life again!" he cried, squeezing
her tightly. "You are not only the best dog in all the land,
you are the most faithful friend I could ever hope for."
Suddenly Jojofu pricked up her ears. She pulled away from her
master and sprang toward the giant serpent. Growling, she put
her nose up to its fat belly and began to claw.
"What is it, girl?" said Takumi, grasping his sword nervously. "Is the
snake still alive?"

When he ran his blade across the serpent's fat stomach, a wide hole opened up and out jumped all the missing dogs! Every one of them ran straight to Jojofu. They jumped all over her, nipping her ears and licking her face in thanks. She barked happily, wrestling and rolling with her friends in the dry forest leaves.

From that day on, Takumi never traveled the forest without Jojofu at his side. They were known by everyone, all across the Province of Mutsu. As they passed through villages, people shouted, "Look! There goes the brave hunter and the dog who slays dragons!" Children stopped Takumi and asked him to tell his tale.

"What is your dog's name?" they would ask.

"Her name is *Jojofu, watashi no me to mimi,*" Takumi always told them.

"Jojofu, my eyes and ears."